140 x 140

140 x 140

Gill James

Chapeltown Books

British Library Cataloguing in Publication Data

A Record of this Publication is available from the British Library

ISBN 978-1-910542-35-4

This edition published 2017 by Chapeltown Books
Manchester, England

All Chapeltown books are published on paper derived from sustainable
resources.

Contents

The Birds and the Bees?

13 May 2014

What? Somebody had gifted him a flowering sponge plant? What was a sponge plant anyway? Somebody else had poked him. There were three friend requests and somebody called Alicia had changed her status. What was the point of this facewhatyoumathingy? It didn't make sense to him.

Then they'd said he should go on Twitter as well and tweet. That was for the birds wasn't it? How would he find that?

"Just start typing it, in Dad," said Rex. "The computer knows."

That's what scared him most of the time. How much the darned machine seemed to know without him having told it.

"I set up your account, Dad." Rex leant over and typed something.

George's face appeared on the screen. Three followers. And there on the right. Who to follow. Gloria Davies. Who'd have thought it?

Damn machine!

Bless it.

Sex Kitten

24 May 2014

Danny opened his eyes slowly. Where was he? Gradually he realised that whatever he was lying on was very hard. Like a floor. He rolled over and his mouth filled with wool. Shag pile.

Shag. Oh Mirabelle. The thought of her made something stir down below. Had they?

He groaned. What was the point if you didn't remember?

Oh, god his head hurt. Snatches of the evening before came back. The heavy metal. Joints being passed round. Tequila shots.

And now there was something staring at him. A monster. A nude man with a cat's head. He shrieked.

"Christ, Danny keep it down. We've all got headaches." Mirabelle stared at his upright cock. "That as well."

There was a loud "Meow" and a small ginger cat jumped out of the carrier bag by the coffee table.

Danny's erection collapsed.

Pastry cooks

7 June 2014

"So what does this do?" Meggie juggled the mouse so that the cursor wavered over the picture.

"It's just the file-name, Mum."

"Oh, so why a cat-flap?"

"It's our cat-flap. I'm programming it so that only Mitzi can use it."

"You're programming it? You don't know how to programme."

"Didn't. Do now." Alice looked up. "Mum, will you quit with all the questions. I've got to get on, you know."

"And you say this is your homework?"

"Yes!" Alice threw her homework diary towards her.

Meggie retrieved it from the floor and opened it. She read the latest entry. "Use your Raspberry Pi to help you invent a useful gadget for your home."

It sounded more like something you might eat for dessert. "Custard tart for pudding?"

"Not hungry. I just want to work with my Raspberry Pi.

Credit

23 May 2014

"You wouldn't be alone," said the man at the bank. "We accept a new customer every four minutes."

Reginald had been sitting at the customer service desk for at least eight. So, that was two more new customers then. Was he supposed to be one of them?

"Don't forget a credit card gives you extra protection. We're liable if a sale goes wrong."

There was that. The blue and white card with the gold chip did look tempting. He'd be able to pay for the holiday upfront. Maybe he'd get the kids some new things. A nice evening dress for Sophia too.

Then he remembered when the bailiffs came and took everything. They'd had to sleep on the floor that night.

"No thanks. Now that I've got my credit record straight."

The bank man sighed. No target meeting today, then.

Trying out

14 June 2014

His dad was waiting for him, just like he did every Saturday after training. Smart shoes. Businessman's overcoat. Cigarette in his hand. Much more elegant than the other dads.

"You did good, son. You showed them who's boss."

"It wasn't a match, Dad. Only a training session."

"Just as important. Don't you forget it. Are you in the team?"

He shrugged. He hoped so. But there was never a guarantee. You had to earn your place.

"You did your best, though?"

He nodded.

His dad slung his arm around his shoulders. "That's my lad."

Dad sighed. "But is your best good enough?"

"I try, Dad."

Dad nodded. "Yeah. Remember even if you don't make it to the team, you playing your hardest makes them do better."

He kissed the photo. He'd done his bit. Now he must wait and see.

Chuck

15 June 2014

Joseph had never seen a chuck like it before. Had it been scared or something? Its feathers were sticking out at odd angles and its eyes bulged. Then it started squawking and running frantically round the yard, as if chased by an invisible monster.

"It's not one of ours, is it?" said Jen.

Joseph shook his head. No, he'd definitely not seen it before.

"Do you think he's come from the Dowden's place?"

"They're not into chucks, are they?" They wouldn't have a clue. In fact, they didn't know much about anything. God knows why they'd bothered buying the old farm.

Jenny moved towards the animal. "Poor thing's scared." She crept up to the chicken, caught it and picked it up carefully. "There now. You're safe here."

She was good with animals. She'd soon have sorted out the Dowden herd.

Preservation

17 June 2014

They'd been going five days now. Five days of blistered feet. Five days of being ignored. Five days of arguing with those who didn't agree.

"Are you all right, Sonia?" Isabelle didn't like the look of her friend. She'd gone grey and she seemed to be having some problems breathing.

"I'm fine. I'll be fine. Something I ate, perhaps." She crumpled and fell to the floor.

"Help. I need some help." Isabelle knelt down next to her friend.

A young man a few feet away took out his phone and pressed three numbers. "Ambulance," she heard him say. He turned to Isabelle. "While we still can."

People were staring.

"Give her some space." The man ushered them away.

Soon they heard the sirens of the ambulance. Then two paramedics were at their side.

"It's all so worth preserving," whispered Isabelle.

Book Launch

21 June 2014

Would that do? The covers were gorgeous but it was certainly a challenge, making books stand out in a library.

"Nice. I hope you get a good crowd." Patsy smiled at her.

"Have we sold many tickets?" Oh no, they'd surely think she was desperate.

"Twelve. Not bad for an event like this. There'll be some footfall as it's a Saturday."

The others walked in. Well, at least they'd have each other for an audience.

"We'll get everybody sat down." Patsy was already ushering people to their seats.

The first row filled up, then the second. Soon, there was standing room only.

"Good turn out," said Colin.

"You go first and get it over with," said June. "As you're the newbie. Then you can relax."

This was it then: she was now officially a writer. She took a deep breath.

Shattered Summer

23 June 2014

There would be dancing in the streets and a carnival atmosphere. The sun was shining and everyone would be out in summer clothes. This was the life. This was the high time.

In the quiet suburbs they set out eager to join in the fun.

"We can park on the edge. Walk in."

"Yeah. Take the tram back and pick up the car tomorrow if we want a drink."

"We might even take a taxi."

They turned into the main road. Nothing coming. All should be well.

They come from nowhere. Two cars seem to race each other. Next comes the sound of metal on metal, then breaking glass, and bodies are thrown around despite seat belts. There is excruciating pain but just for a few seconds. Darkness follows, then light.

And in the city, the party goes on, oblivious.

Alone

4 July 2014

No one else was out. Anyone with any sense was keeping out of the sun. Mad dogs and English men, he thought. What a cliché! But clichés worked for a reason. Everyone knew that. And everyone knew that you didn't walk about mid-afternoon in the summer in towns south of Madrid.

Each step Abel kook made him thirstier. He'd give anything for a cold beer. All of the bars had their shutters down.

Big posters told him that the local cinema was showing a fantasy film and that there was a matinee this afternoon. The auditoriums apparently were air-conditioned. It was just one block away and the big picture started in ten. They would be bound to sell big jugs of cola.

It had come to this, he reflected sadly as he bought his ticket. Going to the cinema alone.

Homecoming

11 July 2014

She slid open the patio door. She could smell the roses. They weren't quite over. It hadn't rained much, they'd told her, whilst she'd been away but even so the grass seemed greener than it had in that arid place she'd just left.

She'd been charmed by his youth and good looks. The sun and sea had made her feel relaxed. Evenings watching the setting sun from the charming terrace had seemed romantic.

But then the conversation had dried up and worse still so did the love-making. The place lost its appeal when the autumn rains came. He visited her less frequently. She suspected he'd found a new love.

She walked to the other end enjoying the spring in the grass. She relished the sea view that she knew she would have later from her work room. She was home.

Don't They?

22 July 2014

"Big boys don't cry," they'd said. Dad was pretty big, wasn't he? So why was he crying?

"Oh, it's only a little scratch, Ben," they said when the tears came.

"If they see you crying they'll do it all the more."

"It's not the end of the world. You'll do better in your next arithmetic test."

Dad was looking at the picture of him and Mum they'd taken just before she became so ill. Dad would probably rather not know he'd seen him crying. Ben crept back to his room but then something jabbed into the bottom of his foot. He yelled. And the tears came.

"Oh, Ben, it's just Lego brick. What are you doing out of bed? Anyway big boys don't cry."

Ben couldn't see any tears on his dad's face. Perhaps big boys don't cry after all.

Booklovers

26 July 2014

Ralph piled the books up on the table. They seemed to be in excellent condition. Maybe she'd picked them for their covers, rather than their content? There were all sorts of colours there: pale blues, vibrant oranges and luxurious golds. Enticing titles, too. *Shadow Princess. Sea Between. The Wilding.* Difficult not to start reading them.

I'll never get this house cleared at this rate, he thought.

What should he do with them? The life-style programmes designated them as clutter, didn't they? And if he wanted to sell Mum's house and his flat in order to buy something bigger… Charity shop or car-boot sale then?

Tobias had climbed on to table next to the books and stared at him defiantly. He'd promised her he'd look after the challenging cat. Ralph sighed. "All right mate, you win. The books come too."

Looking the Part

28 July 2014

What should it be? The old check sports jacket and a flat cap? With a tie? Or maybe something a bit smarter? He took out his dinner jacket. With a dickey-bow, perhaps?

He put it on and gazed at himself in the mirror. Not bad. But not quite right either. It needed something else. A bit of colour or something.

Later, he ambled round the tired seaside town's backstreets. Looking through the junk shops helped him to relax before a show. Sometimes he found new jokes there.

Then he spotted it. It was glorious. A bright red fez with a glistening silky black tassel. He tried it on. It pushed his curls in ridiculous directions.

"What do you want to bother with a silly old thing like that?" his wife asked later. "It doesn't matter what comedians wear. Timing's everything."

Rabbits

31 July 2014

The little rabbit next to the driver was trying to hang on to the steering wheel. He had sun glasses on as well. That showed he was scared.

Why did they always write books for kids with stupid rabbits?

But they did have a picnic in the back of the car – with a proper rug and picnic basket.

If a rabbit could drive a car, so could he. The door to his dad's car was open. Cormy climbed in.

Now, what was it? Foot on one of the pedals and waggle that stick. Then hold on to the steering wheel. "Vrm, vrm."

"Hey, fella. What you're doing?" Dad was holding a rug and a picnic basket just like in the picture. He winked. "Thought we might do the same as your rabbits."

So, those rabbits weren't so useless after all.

Getting into Crime

2 August 2014

Mariese looked at the photo of the dead girl. Why would anyone want to kill someone so beautiful? Pale brown eyes. Creamy skin. Natural gently blond hair, obviously not out of a bottle. Little silver butterfly studs sit prettily in her ear-lobes.

Perhaps that was it though. It was enough to make another woman jealous. Mariese was suddenly reminded of Snow White. She'd been rereading Grimm's fairy-tales. There was an answer to everything, she reckoned, in those stories. No dwarves here, though, she didn't think.

No indeed not. It was the girl's sister who was trying to figure out who killed her. Could money have been a motive? Those ear-studs looked expensive.

Yes. That decided it. She was getting into crime anyway. She slipped this last book into her hessian bag and made her way over to the self-service checkout.

Industrial Revolution

5 August 2014

"Iron horse," she'd heard them call it. God, it must be more powerful than any horse. She didn't trust it though. At the rate they were shovelling in coal it was a wonder the whole thing didn't explode.

Walter's face was red. "She's a beauty ain't she?"

God bless him. He was as excited now as – well the first time they'd been together as man and wife.

"It's going all the way to Liverpool. I could get a job on it. Maybe even drive. They say the pay'll be good." He put his hand on her belly. "And then when the little 'uns start coming we'll have plenty to give 'em."

She hadn't told him that she'd missed her monthly bleeding twice now. Perhaps the iron horse would frighten the baby out of her. They couldn't support a child yet.

The Blue Planet

12 August 2014

It had looked like a peaceful planet as he'd approached. Fertile, too, with great swards of land, some cultivated, some not. Its blueness suggested an abundance of water. It seemed ideal.

They would move in quietly, befriend the intelligent creatures who lived here, gradually teach them their ways. The plan was to live in harmony, for the mutual benefit of the natives and the incomers.

Now, though, he wasn't so sure. Which battle was so important that it scarred the land so much? Mud and ridges. Barbed wire and injured animals. Death and disease everywhere. Who were the inhabitants of this place? Why were they so destructive?

They were not the companions for his peace-loving species. A shame – his people's advanced climatology methods could save this beautiful dwelling.

Reluctantly, he returned to his craft. "Life form not suitable," he reported.

Reading Cat

16 August 2014

That cat was at it again. Being far too intelligent for a cat. His paw moved down the open page, as if he were trying to keep his place, as if he had only recently mastered reading. His eyes, she noticed, were moving slightly from side to side.

"Learned to read have we?" she said in that silly high-pitched voice that humans use for their pets.

"Miaow," he answered. It sounded like "No." No, he'd not learned to read. He'd always known of course.

She tickled him behind the ears.

He shrugged her hand away.

"Nowiaow."

She heard "Not now."

A few minutes later, she heard the cat-flap go. She picked up the book. "Whispers on a Summer Breeze." She looked through the window. His head was cocked as he listened to the flowers' dead heads dancing on the path.

Rebuttal

18 August 2014

They were down there already when she arrived. She hoped they hadn't noticed her. She didn't want to talk to them. There would be the usual silences after everything she said. She found them all so interesting. She must sound dull by comparison.

Some of the lads were already knocking back pints of beer. The girls were sipping red wine from tall-stemmed glasses. She could hear them tittering and making outrageous comments.

There was a bench free near the back door. She sat down and took out her book. She was already half way through it. She was reading too quickly.

"Good story is it?"

She looked up into two dark eyes. Daniel. The one they all fancied and he was taking an interest in her?

"What's it to you?"

He shrugged and walked away.

Fame at Last

20 August 2014

He couldn't believe this moment had come at last. He stood holding up the shirt he would be wearing for the first match. The photographers snapped. Reporters fired questions relentlessly. This was fame, was it?

"Keep cool," the manager had said. "Don't answer the questions. Just smile and be nice."

It had been worth all of those years of training, of playing in the pouring rain on a Saturday afternoon and never having time for what the other young lads were doing. He remembered his father's words. "You'll thank me for this one day."

Then he remembered what his mother had said. "Not too many fast cars. Be nice to the ladies. And don't you start boozing."

It looked as if it was going to be hard work. Despite the glamorous strip. When would he start to have fun, then?

Credit 2

22 August 2014

It was tempting. If he took it, he could get some new clothes, pay Lenny back and treat himself to a takeaway tonight. "No confusing joining offers," said the blurb.

More like they don't want to give too much away. That was banks for you.

That was the other thing though: no credit check. No way would he get a card with his credit history if they checked.

No, he shouldn't. He really shouldn't. Common sense – yes he'd grown some at last – said that if you didn't pay it back straight away they'd whack on the interest.

So, he'd make do with his tattered jeans. Lenny would be patient. Takeaway gave him heartburn even when it didn't cause food-poisoning. Home-cooking was better.

Next month he would have to pay £1000 for his medication: they were closing the health service down.

Magical Reading

24 August 2014

"You can see all right, can't you? Through the gap between that little girl and her daddy in front?" said his mum.

He nodded. There wasn't a lot to see, actually. Just a purple platform with a purple wall behind it. The two pillars at either side looked like golden trees.

"We can get your book signed afterwards."

He looked at the book his mum had bought him on the way in. It had some pictures of a family going into the woods with nets and things.

A lady dressed all in black came on to the platform with a man as old as his granddad. The man started telling a story that went with the picture on his book.

The platform and wall disappeared. The trees became real and he was in the woods with them, looking for bears.

Street Artist

25 August 2014

His fingers were black. He'd been using a lot of dark colours today. This time he was part of a bigger project. And this time he would be paid. Still, though, he kept the basket ready for the coins.

They asked him why he didn't get a proper job. Or even sell more permanent pieces. But this was the way he liked spending his time.

They stopped and admired his work. He skipped round and added a bit of white here a bit of blue there. He'd learned how to care for his back.

"That's it," said one woman. "It's not a puzzle. It's a book about a puzzle."

He concentrated on what he was drawing. He mustn't let her know that she'd got it right.

A coin clinked in the basket. Enough already for a couple of beers tonight.

Supercat

26 August 2014

There was something uncanny about the animal. Sure, it behaved like a normal cat in many ways. It chased pieces of dangling string. It liked every bed more than its own. Boxes were a wonder. And here it was today, trying to get under the duvet with her.

It was a pretty creature. Its stripes were finely drawn and its wide-open eyes made it look at the same time wise like an owl and full of wonderment like any young animal.

Today it was trying to outstare her and had its paws crossed in a meaningful way. Yesterday, she'd caught it in her study sitting on her chair staring at her computer screen.

"What do you want, eh?" She tickled the cat's ears.

"Mee-ow. Ow." He winked, didn't he? He bounded off the bed and back towards her study.

Child Prodigy

30 August 2014

"Wish I hadn't volunteered to drive Olly to the match." I just knew he'd play around with the switches and want some awful channel on the radio. Would Frank get the hint?

"You met his kid yet?" he asked.

I shook my head.

"Well you should. It explains a lot. Go early to pick him up. You might run across the rug-rat."

Two hours later I was standing on the doorstep of the mansion. The maid showed me into the study.

"You here to see my father?" he said. All of four maybe five years, serious glasses, his legs crossed on the foot-rest and reading The Times. God, my kid was still on the reading scheme. "Do you have an opinion on the crisis in Syria? He doesn't."

No wonder his dad got round the office on a pogo stick.

Breakfast Club

2 September 2014

Toby pulled his thin jacket tighter as the wind blasted round the corner of old redbrick building. Why did this have to start all over again? It had been great during the summer. He'd been able to lie in every morning at Grandma's. She'd given him porridge and hot chocolate for breakfast every day. Then he'd been able to play all day with the local kids. There were woods full of adventures near Grandma's.

Now it was back to:

Get out of bed quick.

You might get a glass of milk if you were lucky.

And here's your dinner money that'll only buy junk food.

"Come on in Toby," said Mrs Jenkins. She smiled gently and led him to the school cafeteria. Toby gasped. The tables were laden with bowls of cereal, sausage sandwiches and glasses of juice and milk.

Vocal Chords

3 September 2014

"Go on. It's easy," said Yvette. "No contest. Chocolate, chocolate and chocolate."

"Is chocolate okay for the vocal chords, then?"

Yvette shrugged. "Well dairy isn't. But chocolate's a veg, isn't it? Poof. I don't care. It's cold anyway."

Maddy hesitated. Not for long. Yvette was right. There was no contest. "One scoop of vanilla and one scoop or raspberry," she said as she arrived at the front of the queue.

"Come on, ladies and gents," called Tony. "Let's entertain them while they're in the queue."

She'd better gulp this down quickly then. Not that that was difficult. Not in this heat. A lump of vanilla slid down her throat.

Tony clicked his fingers. "Come on, lets' do it."

She took a deep breath. "When the little blue bird…"

Nope. Raspberry and vanilla were not good for the vocal chords.

39

Rain Passion

6 September 2014

Lightning streaked he sky. The rain came down in torrents.

"Those flashes look like the legs of some sort of alien."

"Yeah. Giant stick-insects or something."

"Thank God. It's cooler now."

Louisa opened the window. "That breeze is so good."

"Mmm." Geri felt the tension dissolving from her body. "I can almost see the grass turning green. And look at the beans. I'd swear they've grown at least an inch since the storm began."

"Mini erections." Louisa rubbed Geri's arm, then allowed her arm to drift nonchalantly up to her neck, skimming her breast on the way. She ran her fingers through Geri's hair.

Geri bent her head so that her lips could meet Louisa's.

"Yes!" Louisa's fingers had found her crotch.

Another flash. Another bang. Geri came for the first time since the beginning of this unbearably arid summer.

Space Projects

9 September 2014

"This is it then. Do you think it will work?"

"Yes. Can't you see it? Keep this part wide open. Leave the beams. The room will go right up to roof. All open plan. Great big kitchen. Plenty of room for the piano. Just think how light will come through those windows."

"Won't it be cold in winter?"

"No, the underfloor heating will warm your feet. That will keep the rest of you warm."

"What about the bedrooms?"

"A wall here. Each bedroom with a big window and a bathroom attached."

The light made her hair look like gold. She shaded her eyes and looked towards the window. Then turned and grinned. It suited her, this place.

They'd bought the loft for next to nothing. His degree in architecture would do the rest. Two great projects starting at once, then.

Procrastination

12 September 2014

She watered the plants, decided the yucca on the stairs needed to lose some leaves, plucked them off and made the whole plant topple. She couldn't leave the soil scattered like that over the carpet.

As she passed through the hallway to get the hoover, the post arrived. Eagerly, she picked up the white and manila envelopes that lay on the mat. Would there be something exciting there?

She down at the kitchen table to read her mail, but only after brewing some coffee. No three book deal. No offer of a writing contract. Not even a rejection slip. Just bills and bumf. Disappointing. She deserved another nice cup of coffee for that.

Hoovering done, she really must get started.

She found the kitten sprawled out across her keyboard. Still no need for her to face the blank page then.

Work Mates

15 September 2014

Jodie feared for Alice's crisp white shirt though envied here her comfortable tartan slacks. *I suppose she has to be comfortable if she's on her feet in the studio all day.*

Alice admired Lindsey's tanned legs. Not smart enough to get her promotion, though.

Lindsey sighed inwardly at Jodie's smart business suit and scraped back blond hair. Why is she is such a hurry to grow up? Susie never managed to.

"Let's do this thing then," said Jodie, "before everybody sets off to work."

Each of the girls took a handful of the coarse dust and scattered it on the water's surface. This was the embankment where the dog-walker had found Susie's body exactly a year ago.

"Sleep well, princess!" Alice tipped the rest of the ashes into the water.

"We miss you." Lindsey blew a kiss towards the river.

Old Habits

16 September 2014

"It's mainly junk. It shouldn't take long." John pulled that hatch open and slid the ladder out.

Tamsin followed him up. She really didn't want this to end. They were leaving the city forever. She wasn't sure she would ever get used to the countryside.

"Do you remember these?" Her violin and his old guitar. "Do you think we can still play them?"

She shrugged but took the instrument and started to tune it. It was in a really good condition, and seconds later she was playing a soft tune. *Your fingers never forget,* she thought.

John tuned the guitar and they played all the old ones. They played on and on until they could play no more.

"We could form a band and tour the local pubs." Perhaps they could. Maybe the countryside wouldn't be so quiet after all.

Clutter

16 September 2014

"Do something. Either they go or I do. You're worse than those hoarders on the telly. Sort it."

Where to start? The cat had jumped over the bedside table, knocking all of the books and his cup of tea over the new soft-pile white carpet. It was a bit mean of her: the books, his precious books, had soaked up most of the tea.

She had a point, he supposed. The "to read" pile on the bedside table was small compared with the one on top of the dresser which was trivial compared with the one on his study floor. Then, all those lining every wall, even the one in the downstairs cloakroom.

"Other people's thoughts," she said. "Can't you think your own?"

He'd get to it in a minute, when he'd read the first pages of Margaret Attwood's *MaddAddam*.

Homestead?

17 September 2014

It looked pretty well set up he thought. There were a hundred houses, all well-constructed and they'd been given a lick of paint. There was the usual saloon bar, the doc's, the store and the chapel. Horses, too, lots of them and men like himself with guns.

It looked robust enough to keep out the Indians.

But would it be good enough for the womenfolk? Was this the place where they could settle?

"Shall we send for the wagons, John?" Dan Boulmer was starting to get impatient.

A shot rang out. It made John jump though he couldn't figure out why; shooting was normal business around here.

"Injuns." Dan reached for his gun.

The Sheriff rode into the square. "All men, armed, to the town edge."

No place for Rose and the little ones, then. Pity. It looked so homely.

Plastic Repair

21 September 2014

Jodie strutted confidently along the street. She would show them. She wouldn't be defeated.

Someone wolf-whistled. She smiled to herself. That, after all, had been the point of the skinny white slacks, the mock leather flying jacket and the stiletto-heeled ankle boots. Don't ever look round. She made sure, however, that her long blond pony-tail swung provocatively and that her heels clopped meaningfully on the pavement: hey, look at me, I'm here.

So, she could still get men to look at her and dream.

"There. It's not perfect and it's as good as it'll ever be. But really not bad at all, considering." She stared at her reflection in the small mirror Dr Mallon was holding. She could see the join where they'd made the repair. She smiled. She rather liked her face like this. God bless poor Henry.

Castle in the Mist

22 September 2014

"Who's stolen the castle?" said John. "Do you remember what a great view we had when we stood in exactly this spot forty years ago?"

"Of course I do." What was he thinking? Who wouldn't remember the first day of their honeymoon – especially on their ruby wedding anniversary?

Everything else had been clear that day as well. He would become a top lawyer. She would become a Headteacher of a village primary school. There would be children and grandchildren. It had all happened. The children and the grandchildren were joining them later in the week.

"You never know." John took her hand and squeezed it. "There might be something else there when the mist clears."

Maybe. It could be fun, this retirement malarkey. You didn't know quite what was going to happen.

The sun peeped through. The castle emerged gradually.

High-rise near the Quays

24 October 2014

It was almost ethereal, this place. All glass and steel, sparkling water and security guards on scooters. Apart from its surroundings. Surreal. Today it was even more so. A special boat made its way up the Ship Canal. Or was it down? It didn't look like a Ship Canal any more anyway.

There were a lot of people on the boat. Out on some jolly, no doubt. Come to gawp at the new world.

"If only they knew," said Greg who had come up from the seventh.

"Yeah." You could see the sprawling council estate from the twelfth. The smashed windows. The burnt out cars. And even the neat front gardens where they'd started to grow vegetables.

"Bet it was a right mess when it was full of wharves, ships and dockers."

"And tarts. Don't forget the tarts."

He wouldn't.

Clichés

1 November 2014

He couldn't see the wood for the trees. He lived by clichés but this was literal. There were so many trees that he had no idea whether he was in the middle, near the edge or even what shape it was. He wondered whether he would ever get out again.

An apt metaphor for the complicated mess his life was. Life? Spinning plates with consequences. Another useless cliché.

He looked a little more closely at the trees. Though they were so closely planted there were leaves and there was evidence that there had been fruit and nuts. The bark was mottled silver and there were intricate patches of light playing round the undergrowth.

Then he realised: he knew exactly where the sun should be and he had a watch.

A quick calculation and he could find his way home finally.

Dressing up

16 November 2014

She unzipped the covers one by one and shook the garments. Yes, these would do very nicely. These would do very nicely indeed. The costumes had the look of steam punk about them and the man's had an added touch of Sherlock Holmes.

They looked like the real thing. If they wore these they could convince the word that time travel was possible, common, even and that time was neither bounded nor impenetrable.

There was a costume each. Tom could dress as the doctor, Sal as the cat woman and Denis as the creepy butler.

People might think they were going to a fancy dress party. There was no time for parties, though. This was business and tonight it would kick off in earnest.

Moments later they faced each other.

"Time to go?" asked the Doctor.

"You bet," they replied.

Flying

22 November 2014

Sandi stroked glitter blusher over her cheeks.

"We need blue lines as well," said Evan.

"And some on the forehead. Both. Make your eyes look big. Look. Like this." She drew an enormous outline of an eye. "And spray your hair. So it stays sticking up." She had pulled her own back into a tight bun.

"Are we good to go?"

Sandi nodded.

"Come on then. One more picture before we hook you up to the harnesses." Dave the Camera was hovering again.

They bent their faces together so that their cheeks almost touched. Almost but not quite.

"Thank you fabbos. Break a leg." Dave grinned.

Hopefully they wouldn't on their first gig after drama school. Flying in front of the town hall to turn on the Christmas lights had its risks, even when you absolutely trusted your non-identical twin.

Black Friday

29 November 2014

Greg was looking forward to a nice cool beer after work.

Black Friday indeed. If they had to have this, why couldn't they have a day off to eat turkey as well?

Still, just half a dozen of the iffy tellies to go, thank goodness.

Oh, that kettle. The woman had swung it round in her excitement and knocked the little old lady out. Poor love. She wouldn't be enjoying her usual fix of Corrie tonight then.

"Oi mate," said the big bloke who'd been in earlier. "This telly's shite. It don't work. I want my money back."

"You get what you pay for," said Greg. "And we have a no refund policy on sale items."

The man lunged and Greg felt his hard fist meet this face. He thought of the little old lady just before he blacked out.

Authorpreneurship

27 December 2014

This woman, he realised, had all the finesse it took. She knew about the art and the craft and even the science of her chosen profession. She knew about the business too. From lonely artist struggling in her garret to car sales woman who took no prisoners with just a dash of lipstick and a flash of glamour. All sorted.

Seven steps, she'd said. The magic of seven. An omen perhaps.

Or was it the glasses that helped, that made her look intelligent?

She was formidable, anyway. Dare he do it?

She was sitting in the lounge of the Rosa Blanca Inn, book in hand. One of his. His stomach flipped. What if she thought it was crap?

She lifted her head sideways. "You know, you really need to take the plunge." She beamed. "Authorpreneurship is the way to go."

Extreme Hangover

1 January 2015

Was this how the New Year was going to start? He'd only wanted to nurse the hangover caused by too much Queen and cheap Spanish brandy. But here he was seemingly trapped in a computer game.

As they got closer he could see they were three men and a woman, all of them with their faces partly covered. They seemed familiar but was that because they were just really clichéd, just what you'd expect in yet another fantasy world vaguely based on something that crossed between Lord of the Rings and mediaeval Europe?

Perhaps he was dreaming and would wake up any second now.

The woman nodded to him. "You remembered, then." Nettie. His estranged wife.

"I'm sure he did."

He cowered as he recognised his father-in-law's voice also. The others were her brothers. His moment of reckoning had come.

Immortal

3 January 2015

"Hold it there. Yes, that's it. Look up towards the skylight." The camera clicked as if it were something from before the digital age. "Sharon, lean back a little further. Go on. You won't fall."

She tipped back as far as she dared. Her hair almost touched the ground now. This would have to be the last gig. She was getting too old for this. Even with the red hair and snakeskin tights. This was going to strain her back even further.

It was odd about Greg, though. It didn't seem to bother him at all. Fifteen years now they'd been modelling together and today he could be mistaken for her son. The red lenses on his shades hid the very small crinkles round his eyes.

Fifty Shades of Gary Vampire was such an apt title. Was that his secret?

Killer Cows

6 January 2015

They always laughed at her when she faced a field of cows and refused to cross it.

"They're talking about me," she would say. "They're going to gang up on me."

"Don't be silly, Renate," they'd reply. "They're just big soppy creatures. They're more scared of you than you are of them. They won't hurt you."

That's what they thought. She knew better, though. These had been bred to kill. Onkel Heinrich had told her so. Let them laugh. She'd be the one laughing when two tons of grassy meat crushed them.

The dark brown one at the far end of the field was looking at her now. It stopped chewing and slowly moved towards her.

The others were still laughing. "Come on Renate. Don't be scared."

Run, she thought. But her feet wouldn't move.

The cow was still moving.

Smile

9 January 2015

The tight reinforced T-shirt gave her little comfort. This was madness. It was all very well for them to pose for the cameras. How could he grin like that? If he did one thing wrong. If he slipped… if she failed to react to him…

She could hear one of the small planes taxiing along the runway. Soon it would be their turn.

What would it be like dying? What, if as you fell, you knew you weren't going to make it and you had to wait for the ground to hit you? What if you survived that but your body was horribly broken?

She took a deep breath. That's why she was doing this. To help mend broken bodies and to give courage to those who couldn't be mended. Like her Greg.

She smiled for the camera.

Morning Commute

12 January 2015

The morning commute at Anytown begins in a whirling dash. Standing room only as the little carriages whiz and stutter in and out of the stations. Stand clear of the doors please. Stand clear of the doors please. Mind the gap. Mind the gap. Train approaching. Stand back.

Heads are bent into the free and paid-for newspapers. They all read the same stories but the thoughts are different. They shouldn't have said that – the reaction is understandable. Such a response is never right. Freedom of speech at all costs.

The train stops. They fold their papers and tuck them under their arms or leave them on the seat for the next passenger. They're not really in this world they share with the other people. Each gradually leaves the setting they've read about as they propel themselves to their working anonymity.

Bookaholic

18 January 2015

Why shouldn't she go in there? She hadn't spent a single penny today. She'd not swiped the plastic once. She'd touched a few jumpers, admired a dress or two and slid her hand, not her foot into some finely sculpted leather. She hadn't been tempted by anything. She couldn't even be bothered.

Here, though, was magic.

Even the name. Moon Lane. Tales on Moon Lane.

Story is more important than possession.

She read mainly electronically these days. Yet, to touch and smell was a rare treat. The souvenir of the story.

And today there was a panda and the man who created it. She must have it. She must key in that pin number once. She could not go home without something.

This would definitely be another one for the collection.

She pushed the door open and it ding-donged obligingly.

Gas Masks

30 January 2015

We looked like monsters when we tried them on. Something that would scare the kids back home. Faces with big eyes and tin hats. Bags hanging from our mouths as if we were horses. What some young lads might imagine was in there, I don't know.

We wondered even if we might scare them, the enemy. Oh, they had their gas masks as well, no doubt. Would they look as scary? Would they be as scared of our gas as we were of theirs?

Then it became comical. We tittered when we realised that, actually, we looked more like clowns than monsters.

When the gas came, though, we were glad of them. Charlie didn't make it. Nor Nev and Jimmy. They just weren't quick enough.

Terrifying when they shouted "Gas, boys, gas," and we struggled to get them on right.

Bears

3 February 2015

"Oh no! Cormy, what have you done?"

He loved that bear with its smart little red check tie. The eyes looked as if they were smiling even though they were only the normal buttons. She doubted whether he would sleep without it.

And now there it was. In the enclosure at the rescue centre. A small brown bear was making its way towards it.

Cormy shook his legs, bounced up and down in his pushchair and giggled.

The bear sniffed the teddy, then jumped back.

Cormy tittered. Next it was on its hind legs and was boxing the toy. Teddy rolled over and she was sure it raised its eyebrows and grinned.

Cormy shook his head and pushed the teddy away when a keeper brought it over to them. "Baby bear need teddy to sleep."

Hmm. But would he?

The Gambler

5 February 2015

Last night it had seemed right. Now he could understand that he had been carried away. Had it been the bubbles in the cheap champagne? He closed his eyes and saw again the red dice. How many times had he rolled them? He could still hear their clatter on the polished tables.

He switched on the computer. He held his breath as it whirred into life. He went to log into his bank account. He got the password wrong twice. Was this an avoidance technique? If he got it wrong again he'd be locked out.

Concentrate. He must concentrate.

He typed in his password slowly.

He was in.

He looked at the account summary. £10,523. He'd got away with it this time.

He opened up his payee list, found Save the Children and typed in £10,000.

Never again. Too risky.

Choices

14 March 2015

Barry's head throbbed. It had been a long week and now it was half past five on Friday afternoon. He had to complete this proposal, though, before he could leave the office.

There was so little to choose between the two ideas that Lauren and Carl had put forward. Both had the normal call to action. One click and the prospect would land on the shopping basket page.

The cleaner hovered near him, impatient to complete his work. Inspiration struck.

"Hey, mate. Twenty quid in it for you if you click one of these buttons."

The man put down his duster and stared at the screen. The mouse hovered. Then, it pointed to a word "click".

Barry handed over the £20.00, saved Lauren's picture, attached the folder to the email, pressed send, grabbed his coat and headed for the pub.

Identity

26 March 2015

You see, Iggy always thought he was a dog anyway. They used to give him dog food to eat. He would drape himself across the back of the sofa while the family watched telly. He liked to roll over and have his tummy tickled. They'd even put a lead on him and led him through the streets. It terrified the inhabitants of Lozells. Other dogs, however, merely barked, just as they would normally whenever they met a known face.

He wasn't exactly the cuddliest of dogs. You couldn't really curl up with him and have a snooze. Nevertheless, he did very well, as pets go.

Still, that iguana had ambitions. It was okay, being a dog. It was promotion for a reptile.

It was the day he started talking and tried to be human that had the family really worried.

Owly Eyes

6 April 2015

You see them all the time, don't you? Those males with owly specs: Harry Potter, Clark Kent, my mum's first husband. They all surprise you. Either they take on everyone's nemesis and good overcomes evil, or they do a twirl in a conveniently located telephone box and they save the world or they simply belie their nerdy looks and turn out being brave and victorious.

All of this made Marcus such a disappointment. He'd always looked kind of cute, actually, and these days those wire-rimmed specs are a fashion statement. Understated, I suppose.

I waited and waited to be swept off my feet but nothing happened – until the day I stamped on the wretched things.

He called me a bitch but then we had the best sex ever.

So, the way to a man's heart is through his broken specs?

The Writer's Lot

9 April 2015

In the mirror I see a man at an end of sorts. He seems not to be in this world. It's probably the exhaustion, the brain deadness and knowing that it's nowhere near right. But they're done now. I've finished the first eight drafts.

Tch! Writing is all rewriting they say. I remember scoffing at that. "You're kidding me. Surely, just write it and polish it a couple of times?"

Naw. Check for one thing each edit. I have a personal list of eighteen. Read it out loud. Get someone else to proof read. And you'll still want to twiddle post-publication. I know these things now. I've put in my 10,000 hours.

It'll get better soon. Draft number 9 begins to look like literature.

Next time I look in the mirror I'll see a man with hope in his eyes.

Democracy

15 April 2015

The white card with his name on mocked him. He felt slightly sick every time he looked at it. This was a huge responsibility. What if he got it wrong?

"Have you made your mind up, yet, son?"

He shook his head.

His father frowned. "Only a few days left now. Don't waste it."

His mother came into the room. "He's right. You mustn't. Your great-grand mother went to prison so that women could do this. It galls me to see a disinterested man."

His father snapped his briefcase to. "Get reading. Or watch the debate again. It's still on the Sky box."

They left. He envied their work routine and he resented still having to live with them. Who would give him a chance? None of this lot!

What to do? Go by colour perhaps? Blue was his favourite.

Plastic Revenge

17 April 2015

She shuddered when she saw it. A grey sky and a threatening storm drained the landscape of colour. It made it look like a poster for an old black and white horror film. Its towers and turrets were like clichéd reminders of what she was running away from.

She's a witch. She put some sort of spell on him. Bitch more like.

The taxi-driver cleared his throat. She smiled as she proffered Nigel's credit card. Oh, yes, she would bend this a bit this weekend.

The sun came out as she walked up the steps into the lobby. Colour burst forth. It was all a sham after all. The thick carpet and shining wood veneers said refurbished 5* luxury. Oh yes, this would cure her alright – and possibly kill him when the bill came in.

Beggars

27 April 2015

"We should make a move," said City Gent.

"Oh, let's wait a while longer." A group of women passed by. Yes, he was right. There were rich pickings here. The girl in the pink Gingham dress fished a fiver out of her purse.

Gladius stuffed it into his shirt pocket. "Gents, we have enough for a decent supper now tonight."

Albi took a swig from his flask in celebration. He was now getting quite adept at working round his alien mask. He offered it to me. I put the top to my lips. The liquid was hot and made me tingle as it went down.

Albi pointed up to the sky. It looked like Albi, only this time with wings.

"Who is it?" I whispered.

Gladius nodded at City Gent. "Let's go. Charlie's hallucinating. Let's get him away from the crack."

Swimming

3 May 2015

I dreamt that I was a mermaid. That I could float gracefully through the sea and that I danced with the waves and the seaweed. My long blond hair crinkled in the water. I swished my tail and propelled myself efficiently just above the bottom.

You wanted to join me. You called to me in the night, so I came to fetch you. You still had your PJs on for you were really asleep. I had to hold you firmly or you might have floated away and I'm not sure you can swim. This is my time, but I was glad to have you with me for a while.

Now I'm back in my chair, tailless with two legs that hurt. A little less today though. And look. How nice. Someone's painted a picture of the sea-bed on the wheels.

House Fire

12 May 2015

The flames were glorious. Bright orange and roaring they licked the black sky. A middle-aged man was watching. He was deadly pale and glowing with sweat. He chewed at his lip.

"Who lives here?" I asked.

"A couple of unmarried sisters. Quite old they were. And a bit doddery. They should have gone into a home a long time ago. One of them probably left the stove on. Accident waiting to happen if you ask me."

Another fire truck arrived. "Have they recovered yet?" I heard an officer say.

"No, but they're expecting fatalities. The crew'll be out soon. It's been too long."

I watched for the hour it took them to put out the fire. They brought out the bodies.

Later, I saw his picture on Twitter. Arrested on suspicion of arson and the murder of his two aunts.

Twins

18 May 2015

The greyness lifted as soon as I walked through the door. The pictures on the wall and the flowers on the table said that this was our sort of place. And she was already sitting there, my twinny. We'd not met for a while. She'd been overseas. I'd missed her.

We chuckled. Different books, yes. But similar, definitely.

"I read that three weeks ago," she said.

"Shit. And I read what you're holding before I started on this one."

"God. How do we do it?"

"Genetics over environment, then?"

She shrugged. "Arguably we're in one big samey environment."

Maybe she had a point. Manchester. New York. What was the difference? They obviously both sold classy brown shirts.

"So what was the best bit?" I asked.

I expected stories of mega-shopping, handsome dates and impressive deals.

She smiled softly. "Finding nothing's changed."

Brothers

21 May 2015

No one realises. We are in fact brothers, destined to confront each other perpetually. I look again into his red tortured eyes. I see the pain and the anger. It must make him wretched. He rarely sees the light and breathes mainly sulphur. His eyes have grown small from seeing in the dark.

He has more muscle than I. Most would consider him stronger. I guess he gets the practice as he hops around causing mischief. Mine is a gentler way. I use kind words, gentle persuasion and good examples. He is all fun and victory.

"Come on then, old softie, show what you're made of. Our loving father won't help you now."

He grins.

I feel guilty for being our father's favoured son.

Can we do it? Settle at last the war between good and evil on an arm-wrestle?

Sisterhood

22 May 2015

I was a little afraid to open the book. Silly, really. I'd wanted to read it for ages. What was it going to tell me though? Would it confirm what I already knew? What I feared, in fact. That these young women were there just to serve men?

Oh, it wasn't a nasty slavish thing. It was more subtle. Would they remain young women, though? Would they have anything of themselves?

I opened it.

It was a work of beauty. It spoke of beautiful things too. Of rich linens, fine embroidery, of cosy family meals.

There was a bulge towards the end of the book. Something seemed to stick between the pages. As I opened the page, something pricked me. A pressed rose as a book mark.

Suddenly I saw her. Not a slave, but a lover. Adored and cherished.

Homecoming

3 June 2015

The stark bleakness of it all suited my mood. Those dark clouds up above turned everything into shades of grey. Then, there it was suddenly, the place we used to call home. It was still intact. The windows weren't broken. The door looked safe. I even thought I could see smoke coming from the chimney. Someone was at home.

Only a few more metres now. Beyond the little house I could see the rest of the city, lights now showing through some of the windows. It was June and only four o'clock in the afternoon but it seemed dark already. Would I get there before it started raining again?

A light snapped on in what I knew to be the kitchen. They must have known I was coming. Which one of my noisy family had been patient enough to wait?

Beach Read

10 June 2015

The shop was shady, providing some welcome relief from the hot sun that made walking unbearable and left you ever thirsty. A less pleasant musty smell spoke of old books, slowly burning paper and words mixed with stains of sun-tan lotion and beach cocktails.

Never mind all of that. He needed something to occupy his mind. Funny, he thought, seeing everyone there on the beach with their paperback or their e-reader and actually not there at all, but all in totally different worlds.

He looked for a name he knew and found none. Next he looked at the covers. Now, this was interesting. An antique sword and swirls of fire. Hints of conspiracies, secrets and ancient prophecies.

Similar, actually to a family beach holiday after all.

He paid his three euros and made his way back, smiling, to his sunbed.

Bergen Belsen

12 June 2015

They'd entered the camp early, just after it got light. What a way to start the day! There were bodies everywhere. The smell made some of the men vomit. His medical training protected him from that. It also made this all the more unbelievable, though.

"How can they be alive when they're that thin?" asked Tom.

He was not a medical man like Jack and yet Jack couldn't have put it better himself. What was more astounding? That humanity could stoop so low or that it could be so resilient. Even today the thought of the striped uniforms sickened him.

He was getting frail now and his own life would end soon. His heart had grown large. If he could have his time again he would be a pacifist. Such cruelty surely came from the same instincts that allowed war.

Why do we read?

16 June 2015

"She should be doing something with her hands. Making something. Producing something. What's the good of stories? Filling her head with that nonsense."

My grandmother's normal mantra. What she always said. She never understood about books and learning.

I didn't get it either. I loved reading, now that I'd discovered the library. My teachers were pleased. Even back then reading was my default activity.

Yet grandmother was right, I thought. What is the point of reading?

My son is taking ages to choose his picture book. He looks at every single one every time we come here. He knows the stories inside out and back to front.

"This one," he says at last.

It's the one about the wicked pirates. Again. A startlingly dark one but sitting cosily on the bed and reading the pictures together isn't dark at all.

Karma

8 July 2015

What to choose. She had no idea. It would have almost been easier if there had been no choice. She settled in the end for the moules marinières with fresh-baked brown bread. They were of course delicious: the hint of butter, the white wine, the saltiness, the flat-leaf parsley. The taste of the sea took her away from the greyness of Manchester.

She paid and left.

"Spare a few coins, ma'am?" said the guy sitting in the shop doorway with his dog.

She ignored him.

"Have a nice day," he called.

She kept on walking, her eyes fixed on an invisible horizon, ignoring the young mother with two children under five scrabbling in the food bank.

Not her fault. Nothing she could do about it.

The heartburn kicked in as the tram arrived at Piccadilly Gardens. Her punishment, she supposed.

Expat

15 July 29th

They said the black coffee, the raw tobacco and the fierce sun were bad for him. What about the slower way of life, the fresh food and the lack of aches and pains, though? And his pension went further than at home.

John and Elizabeth were going to pop by later. These visits from old friends were becoming infrequent. Now he was kind of sad. Not that he missed the hassle. But friends were dying one by one.

They had aged more than he had, he thought.

"You must miss her, though," said Elizabeth.

He did, a little.

"It must be difficult when you haven't got your friends around you," said John.

They looked even older when they struggled to get into their car later.

No, he wasn't lonely. He met his chums under the lemon trees every morning and evening.

The Couch

16 July 2015

Purple could be for the young as well as the old. It was for the powerful. Wasn't it a colour of royalty also?

This was luxury. This showed his status. This was what he deserved.

"I suppose you'll be even more of a couch potato now! And why you had to pick that God awful colour I don't know."

Well it was the only one left at half price, buy now and start paying in twelve months' time. Interest free credit.

She jumped into the space beside him. "It is comfy, though, but I'm not sure how long I can stand this colour."

She was right. It was really gross. Well, he'd show her he wasn't a couch potato. He'd just have a little snooze before he got started on painting the walls grey or silver to set it off.

Magic

4 August 2015

There was nothing but trees as far as he could see. Thankfully there was sunlight coming through. He kept on walking. Surely if kept on going south he would come to an end eventually. The sun would guide him.

"Arthur, give me the throne and you will be free of this place." The voice of his half-sister. He knew, though, that he was only imagining it. There was no such thing as magic any more. His father had banned it.

They had played together as children. They had learnt to hunt and to fence together. He's been so proud that she was as good as him. Why did he see her like this now?

Something moved in the trees. Was that an old man with a long white beard? No, nothing.

Suddenly he was at the edge of the forest.

Gourmet Breakfast

11 August 2015

She had dreamed of this. Getting up lazily but no too late. Finding the first bright café-bistro and ordering breakfast. No work to get to today. No office to check into. Just all that creative stuff waiting for when she was ready. No one else to please.

This one looked good. It had dark oak chairs, white tablecloths and an excitingly long breakfast menu.

She took her seat. The waitress arrived. She ordered coffee and orange juice to start and studied the menu.

That would do: the burrito with scrambled egg, baby tomatoes and mixed peppers. Served with strawberry relish and sour cream.

It looked colourful on the plate when it arrived. The coffee and juice were good too. It was just a shame there was no one to share it with. She was suddenly aware of her acute loneliness.

Software

It really stressed him out. Every time he went to do something there was some new technology, new software to learn, more social media routines to embrace.

"You must always try out the beta system," they told him. "It's so much easier to put right than to wait until the real one's out. Stops us getting egg on our faces."

He clicked through to the web site from his phone. The post was huge, 1,000 words he reckoned. He scrolled down. The pictures didn't help. They terrified him.

Some people have got too much time. You just got used to one thing and they brought in another.

He walked along the A6. The traffic whizzed by. The Irwell was just down there. Should he? Yeah, go on. He slung the phone over the parapet. Result. *Now go.* Peace at last.

Fraud?

24 August 2015

They expected her to be wise. She was a good writer. Everyone knew that. They expected her to teach them.

She sat down at her keyboard. She bit her lips. Words failed her.

No such thing as writer's block, she told herself. Was her work in progress failing?

Come on, you know what to do. He must learn his lesson. It will make him grow as a person. What is it? What is it?

She missed the cat. He was out hunting. Who could blame him? There were field mice about in August, exposed after the hay-making. Did he really help her? Was it now a superstition?

She sighed. Good job she used an avatar for her social media. Good that they couldn't see her all sweaty and stressed.

Come, she told herself. Walk your talk. Get down to it.

Gods 26

17 August 2015

She was a magician. She would conjure up people and haunt them with their own pasts. She had the control. She was their god. What if she herself were just a character in somebody else's story? It was all preordained. It was all written.

But wait, no. They began to take on a life of their own. They began to take paths she hadn't chosen for them. Sometimes she wished they wouldn't do this or that and knew they would get themselves into trouble.

They did. Occasionally they looked shyly for her help. She would set them back on their feet, tap them gently on the head and send them on their way, whispering "There there. All better now."

This was the power of prayer, she thought, the power of intercession and she in turn then voiced her own prayers.

New Pathways

27 August 2015

It was coming to an end. That dream time. That time of being so absorbed in what you were doing that you didn't notice what you were doing. Yet you knew you were learning, you were changing and you were having fun. But what would happen next?

So now, one day after lunch, we gathered around our laptops and followed a link we'd never seen before.

"That's what Jinglebabs used to bang on about. Shall we take a look?"

I nodded. It was a path we'd never been along before. Like in the Devon countryside, you can't see round the next corner because of the high hedges.

We found Pandora's box. So many things to do, places to go, people to meet.

"Time to dust off the old CV," said Tim. "Have you ordered your graduation robes, yet?" asked Alice.

Bookaholic 2

17 September 2015

"Did you get the shoes?" Marcia asked.

He shook the contents of the bag on to the table.

Marcia gasped. "You won't be able to keep your feet dry with those. You've got holes in your old ones. What are you going to do?"

He shrugged. He hated clothes shopping. He always came back with a book instead.

She picked one up and flicked thought the pages. "It smells of new book," she murmured.

He laughed. "Of course. What do you expect?"

He picked one of them up and plunged his face between the pages. Yes, there we a glorious newness about them.

"Your poor feet though." She shook her head and moved towards the kitchen. She sighed. "I'll make some tea."

He stacked the books neatly on the table. He bit his nail. Which one would he read first?

Observed Time and Elapsed Time

5 October 2015

She had thirty minutes that was all. She knew her hair looked elegant. Scraped back, it showed off her shoulders and neck. She smoothed the cream into her golden tan. She'd worked on that. She hoped he would be impressed.

She looked at the clock. Barely thirty seconds had gone by. Observed time was always slow to pass.

She'd look surprised, still wrapped sexily in her towel. She'd comment that he'd got there earlier than she'd expected.

She remembered the short story she'd downloaded the night before. Thirty minutes, the guy had said, to read and one minute to review.

Soon she was absorbed. So much so that she hardly heard the key in the lock and the footsteps on the stair. She blushed as he opened the door.

"Just give me a minute. I need to write a review."

Cookery Contest

8 October 2015

It's all over now. We've weighed and mixed and stirred. We've tried to keep our touch light. We've carefully chosen unusual ingredients. We've prayed as the ovens hummed. Our friends and family have watched. Strangers talked about us. The judges will judge. The winner will be announced any second.

One by one the others had to leave the game. It's like that a lot, isn't it? On TV shows at least. Good job real life's not the same. Or is it?

There they are. She prods my neighbour's sponge. He draws a breath as he sees my tower of raspberry-lined gateaux.

There are murmurs.

"Eye-catching."

"Intriguing."

They sample forkfuls.

"Hmm. Delicate."

"Exquisite flavour."

The seconds tick by, seeming like hours.

Why do I do this?

She puts down her fork and smiles at the camera. "And the winner is—"

Afterlife

17 October 2015

It wouldn't be long now. He was certainly getting to the end of his allotted number of heartbeats.

None of it had been that bad actually. It had been a good life. All that he could have ever wished for, actually. Even this illness had been bearable. He just hoped, though, that when the time came it would happen in his sleep. That he'd just not wake up.

Something niggled though.

He picked up the book from his bedside table. It was damned good. Even though he was weaker now and reading was a struggle, it gripped him.

He shuffled himself around so that he could prop himself up on one elbow and hold the book open with the other hand.

Yes, this was great. And he should have written his book. Now he had to believe in an afterlife.

Hacker

16 October 2015

She was transfixed by the figures in the little charts. All blue. Blue meant left-braindedness, science, mathematics. She always associated blue with maths. Her maths exercise books at school had been blue.

"Don't just be fascinated," she mumbled to herself. "Study them properly. Make them work for you."

She looked more closely. This wasn't just a financial prediction. It was showing how much crime was going to pay. Or rather, how much it was going to cost.

Suckers, she thought.

It was her job after all, to hack into thing like this, to prove that their security was inadequate. Or maybe she should try something new?

She hesitated.

She smiled to herself.

Then her fingers started flying across the keyboard. Soon she was in.

She watched as millions transferred into her secret bank account. She would be rich very soon.

Taking Mum's Advice

25 October 2015

The best way to find out about any city, his mother had always told him, was to walk around it. Become acquainted with the people who live there. Find out its quietest secrets. She'd not meant go on a guided walk aimed at tourists.

The girl in the office was persuasive: "You don't get a truer picture than when you only travel by tube."

So here he was, standing on the corner of Baker Street, looking for Sherlock. The others were just the sort of tourists he hated. They were looking for quick unsubstantial thrills. But then she arrived. The girl with the green eyes and the heart-melting smile.

His mother's word haunted him. "It's the only way you'll get to know the people."

The girl smiled. Her name was Fiona, he noted. He'd like to get to know her.

Nostalgia

28 October 2015

So different now, from all those years ago. Granted, it was summer then and now it was autumn going on winter. Even so, back then, there would have been children on the beach, getting some fresh air in their half term holiday.

Snap.

Yes, it was a digital camera, but it still made the sound of the shutter going. He smiled. He wasn't the only one who indulged in nostalgia.

It was eerily beautiful here. The dunes were recovering because nobody walked on them much these days.

He must capture it all. The ivory softness of the sand. The grey blue of the sea and sky. The cries of the seagulls. Snap. Snap. Snap.

The red telephone box took him by surprise. There weren't many left, he thought. He went in and dialled. She answered. He thought he was dreaming.

Gifts

6 November 2015

"So, what do you give a man who has everything? Who is so old and wise he wants and needs nothing or so he thinks?"

Lucie shrugged her shoulder and shook a head. "Maybe a personalised number plate? He does drive, still, doesn't he?"

"Hmm." Not bad. Vi was glad she'd asked her niece. That girl was full of ideas.

She started spotting them on the way home. PJC KS3. G1LL 45, 1 CUR64. Nothing wrong with giving a person's age away, it seemed.

What might they have though? Looking through the list was fascinating but she couldn't find anything about football or computers.

The big day came. She held her breath as he unwrapped the oblong parcel.

His eyes grew round and he chuckled. "Indeed I am and yes I can."

She nodded as she read again: R77 SEE.

Too shy

11 November 2015

He fell in love with her at once. She was beyond sexy. The parted lips, the long black hair and the penetrating stare all fired him up. Some, he knew, would say it was just lust. He knew, though, that there was more to her than just a few random charms.

He watched her working with the children at the Kindergarten. They loved her too.

He hesitated each time he tried to connect. Not knowing seemed better than disappointment.

There were three botched attempts. He took her chocolates and gave them to his daughter Tanya. He went to ask her out but then talked about Tanya's maths. He tried to be friendly but let a bossy mum dominate the conversation.

One day he saw another loved-up dad give her a rose and was sad at the way her face sparkled.

Power Cut

3 December 2015

Thirty-six hours and ten minutes. That was how long he'd spent on answering the questions, boasting about himself – though he didn't like boasting – and making the best case possible.

In two hours he must press the 'send' button. Would they be convinced? Would they give him the money for the girls' programme? Educate the women and all will be well?

He checked the answers carefully and ran over the figures again. It was a good job that he had a gift for numbers. Yes, all was well.

One last break, then, before he sent merrily it on its way.

As he switched on the kettle the lights went out.

"Yes, it's a power cut," said the voice on the end of the phone. "We've actually run out of energy. We estimate that the power will be back within three hours."

Dreams

13 December 2015

He couldn't make it out at all. He usually knew what dreams meant but not today. Who were these people and what did they mean? The strong rugby player looked as if he were about to run with the ball. Maybe run forever not just towards a scrum. The girl carrying the bird-like puppet seemed very young and actually rather attractive. Was that her father? Older brother? Uncle? Future husband? He seemed hostile? Was he about to attack?

The warrior's eyes rolled to the back of his head and he began to shake. The girl started chanting. The other villagers joined in.

"Hey," called the rugby player. "Catch, man."

Toby caught the ball without any problem.

"Now, run. You've got to leave this all behind you."

The warrior fell.

Toby suddenly knew that his try-out later today would go well.

Chocolates

14 December 2015

The tin still looked full but she'd already found some empty wrappers. Still, they hadn't been too greedy. Then she worried. Teenagers refusing chocolate could be a sign of other problems.

It wouldn't hurt to have just one would it? As a treat for finishing her marking. She rummaged through the tin. Hmm. Not a lot of choice after all. Yes, she remembered Belinda had piled up all of the ones in the purple wrappers. There were a lot of sickly strawberry creams. Now, if they'd been an infant school class no doubt most of those would have been gone.

Then she spotted it, the triangle wrapped in green paper. It must be a sign that she'd been right after all to treat her students and stop for a moment worrying about bribery and the onset of diabetes or obesity.

Marking

21 December 2015

The first assignment he tried to mark looked nothing like a script.

"She's centred it," he mumbled to himself. "Centred every single speech." That would never even get looked at in the film world.

The second was a little better. At least the dialogue was set out correctly. However, the scene heading wasn't in block capitals. That wouldn't do either.

A third was almost perfect. Yet even here, damn it, the parenthetical information wasn't centred correctly.

He read through fifty or so more and despaired of finding the perfect script. One more, he thought, before he called it a night.

There it was then. The beauty. The one that made it all worthwhile. Absolutely spotless.

He'd failed no one. There were some good stories. Could he give this one 100%?

He sighed. Probably not. His colleagues would never allow it.

Status

24 December 2015

"A barrister, eh? Not bad. He seems terribly young. How long's he been doing that for?"

"A couple of months now."

"How long did it take him to qualify?"

Naomi shrugged. She didn't know and she didn't care. Clearly, though, her mother did. Always the same story. Always the same unspoken question. Is this the one you're going to marry? Is this the one who will be the father of my grandchildren?

"He's good at it. That's all that matters, isn't it?"

He mother sighed. "I suppose so. As long as you're happy and he can support you."

"Mum! I've only been seeing him a couple of months."

"Coffee's up!" Rudolpho beamed at them as he placed down the tray. The three cappuccinos were adorned with stars and a decorated Christmas tree.

"I told you he was good," whispered Naomi.

Memory

2 January 2016

Greg went hot and then cold when he recognised the implications of what the Commander had just said. The man steering the attack-craft was none other than his own son. In less than twenty minutes Tom's vessel would crash into earth and release a poison cloud that would kill thousands and leave much of the planet inhabitable for decades.

What had got into the lad? Could he do anything to change his mind?

"Patch me through," he said to the communicator.

The young man nodded. "Go ahead."

"Tom. Remember Fairley."

Greg's own memories almost choked him. Melissa had still been alive then and they'd all enjoyed playing on the sand and swimming in the sea.

Tom's face flickered. He reached forward to touch the controls.

"Go on," Greg urged. "You know what's right."

Tom closed his eyes. The engines stopped.

Failed Artist?

6 January 2016

Yet another offer. Yet another promise. One more suggestion that it is possible to sell. That's all he seemed to do these days. Market, market, market. Promote, promote, promote. But selling?

Neither was he producing anything. He kept staring at a blank canvas. Literally.

"Your work is good. Even very good," the man at the gallery had said. "But there are so many more like this. It just lacks some sparkle. There is no soul to it."

He'd poured his heart and soul and other clichés into this work. What did this little man know?

He would have to go back to emptying dustbins. That at least would pay the rent and cover the food-shopping.

It was as he loaded the last bin that he noticed the swirl of colours and he knew what he would paint next: vibrant rubbish.

Change of Fortune

9 February 2016

She was tired of going to work and coming home in the dark. She was glad to be escaping to the south for a couple of days. It would rain less, there'd be more blue sky and the days would be that bit longer.

Then suddenly Robert was standing in front of her. He was wearing a T-shirt with the name of a jewellery shop on it.

He grinned. "See. I told you something would turn up."

Those weeks of being unemployed had shattered him. Now, though, he looked full of life.

He handed her an envelope. "Pretend you don't know me in case you get lucky."

She opened it later. A £50 voucher and some pictures of gorgeous rings and pendants.

The conference would soon be over and she'd be back to their cosy joint life in Rainy City.

Book Nerds

10 February 2106

"Don't you want to go and play football with the other guys?"

"No, Mum. I'm fine here."

Alice didn't like it. He never seemed to hang out with other kids. She ought to be grateful, really. He was reading and doing it very well for his age. His teacher had said so. Even so, she wished he wasn't so lonely.

Late, as she prepared supper, he startled her.

"Mum," he said all breathless and excited. "I want to start a club."

"A club?"

She'd never seen him as excited this. Deeply interested in the books on the shelves in the bookshop or the library. But excited, no, never.

"So who would join this club?"

"Harry. Ben. Daniel."

"And what would it be about?"

"Books of course. We'd be the Nerdy Book Blub."

She smiled and nodded. That figured. Great news!

The Book of Chemical Constants

13 February 2016

She had forgotten it. The book of chemical constants may have been boring, and water-damaged, and sold very cheaply in an independent bookshop but its main purpose always, as far as she had been concerned, was to press flowers. Excellent it was too, for here was the rose, white and still looking like a perfect rose.

What had made her look? Some desire to declutter the house in case they decided to move? Why had she taken it off the shelf?

It was heavy and awkward and tumbled to the floor, scattering the rose on to the carpet.

Yes, Valentine's Day, forty-one years ago. He'd put a white rose on her desk. She knew it was him. And every year since, a card, with a note in his hand-printing, saying "From guess who".

She wondered what tomorrow would bring.

Fabrics

14 February 2016

The rows of fabrics dazzled her. She wanted to touch them. There were cottons, softer woven jerseys, linens that creased easily and smooth silks that she wanted to hold next to her skin. Best of all though were the soft velvets.

What to choose though? And what did she want to make first? A roomy top to cover her growing belly? Something exceptionally cute for the son she knew was going to arrive in a few weeks' time?

"What about that?" Her mother pointed to a yellow gingham. "A safe bet. It'd do for a girl or a boy."

She shook her head. She didn't want to be safe. "This I think." She took a large piece of shocking pink velvet out of the remnants' box. "And that too." She picked up a bright orange felt silhouette of a duck.

Alert

18 February 2016

Bizarre. They were there yet they were in other worlds. Some had their heads in a book. Others had ear-buds plugged in. Just a few like him simply daydreamed. No one knew what the others were thinking.

The train lurched as it crossed the points. It recovered its balance and carried on.

It was normal. The route was always the same. He looked at the same faces every day. They passed the same buildings. He would get off at his normal station and walk along the four hundred yards to his office.

Then though he noticed three men speaking rapidly into their handsets.

He wasn't surprised when the huge explosion happened though he was glad he'd been a little bit alert and not lost in another world. At least he was able to find his way out of the carriage.

Winter

19 February 2016

Most definitely colder than home but also clearer. Land snow-cleaned white and the sky and the lake blue-grey. No one except her there. Her sides ached as she breathed in. She'd better keep moving or she'd freeze.

The snow slowed her. It didn't hurt if she fell though it did make her coat wet and that made her colder. Walking warmed her but robbed her of her breath.

She took one step and then the next and the next after that. She was getting there.

At last the inn came back into sight.

She pushed the door open. Would they all be there yet?

She heard laughter. She smelled the strong coffee and the freshly baked bread. The landlady smiled at her.

She turned once more to look at the pristine landscape and worried that her footsteps had broken it.

Heat

21 February 2016

The heat was almost unbearable. She had to cover her face. Yes she couldn't help looking at the red hot rock. She could just make out that it was flowing.

"They actually cook the meals on it you know," said Toby. "Would you like try it?"

She shook her head. She wasn't hungry.

What might it feel like if you fell into that hotness? How long would you feel the pain for? How long would it take to die?

He touched her arm gently. "You've got to eat, you know. Some time you've got to start living again."

She looked at the fence. It wasn't high. It would be easy enough to scramble over it.

"Come on." He started to lead her away.

"Okay. Let's go to the restaurant."

He smiled.

At least, she thought, the wine would numb her.

Baftas

27 February 2016

Lists of names scrolled past endlessly. She recognised a few, so called those out anyway. If she knew them, that must mean something. They'd made their impression. She tried to beat her colleagues to it. The headset pinched and she had a sharp pain behind her eyes.

First came the actor who had made her debut in a ground-breaking psychological thriller. Yes, good.

Then there was the director who had really managed to get the view into suicidal young man's head. Go on. Give him a go.

That elderly actor was impressive too. The next Gielgud perhaps.

Then, though she spotted it. Yes, the young actor who took all of the impish teen parts. He would certainly go far. He would be on these lists every year.

She called out his name. The room became silent and her headache lifted.

Defiance

18 October 2016

It was still her favourite colour, even though she was grown up now. Yet it was years since she'd worn anything so softly coloured. She hadn't been out for months. She'd never worn a hat before.

She looked in the mirror. It would do nicely. Her hair had grown back quickly but patchily. The hat hid the bald spots. The rest of her hair hung impressively at either side of her face.

"You ought really to have had it cut," the Macmillan nurse had said. She'd refused. Losing one boob had been bad enough. She didn't want to lose any more femininity.

Yes, her lipstick was the same shade of pink. Her eye makeup stopped her eyes looking tired. The dangly earrings gave her a hint of glamour.

She stepped out into the street and the boy next door wolf-whistled.

About War

19 October 2016

"War is hell," he says. "It's not terrible. It's awful. If the heads of state can't agree, you send young people to kill other young people they don't even know, who may never have harmed them or anybody else."

There were facts which would have seemed incredible. We say, don't we: "They can't be doing that. It's not humanely possible."

He went, 27, as a liberator into the camps, not as a visitor. It was all rats, lice, dysentery and other diseases.

There were 22 seats in the docks. Three thousand could have been tried for the same crimes.

"Law not war is the answer," he claims. You'd save so much money you'd be able to take care of the students who can't pay their tuition, take care of the refugees who don't have homes. "Never give up," he adds.

Survival

20 October 2016

The sea roared behind them. They could still hear the creaking of the ship they'd abandoned. She would go down any moment.

"We'll have to ride the waves," called the skipper. "Just go with the flow. No point in fighting it."

This was Tommy's fifth storm and he'd only been sailing for three months. It was the most frightening of all even though they were in view of land. He gripped on to the side of the rowing boat as best he could. He was shivering so much he thought he would have to let go soon. What would his ma and his brothers and sisters do if he died?

A great wave came, almost tipping them out. He clung on. Then they tumbled on to the smooth flat sand just as the sun began to peep though the clouds.

Statistics

20 October 2016

He looked at her charts and smiled. You could make a lot of this, he told himself. And you could also make a lot else out of it as well.

"You see," said the presenter. "We're in a period of growth. Income is up by 25% on last year and expenditure is down by 10%. We look set to make a good profit this quarter."

He raised his hand. She nodded to him.

"What will happen if we don't sustain that growth? And why aren't we reinvesting our profit?"

A cloud passed across her face. "It's essential that we maintain the growth. We do intend to use our profit to buy more personnel to accommodate our growing client base."

A week later she started her presentation with considerable concern. "If we don't maintain these figures, we'll be looking at redundancies."

Colours

23 October 2016

Pink beads today, the only choice. Val always took her time to get the exact match for her clients. Yes, pink, with a touch of grey. A pale pink. The beads would still catch the light.

Annie had had to go into a nursing home the day before. She had always been a gentle soul so she didn't complain. She didn't complain either about being pipe-fed now. No more roast dinners. Not more chocolate puddings.

"We might be able to get her off that," said the manager. "We do sometimes."

Annie's daughter had shaken her head and turned to Val. "I don't think so. Will you make her something to cheer her up, please?"

So there were all the beads, and the string and the catch. Val selected a triangular bead with more grey than pink to start it off.

The Hooded Samaritan

24 October 2016

He never showed his face. He always pulled the top of his hoody so far forward that you couldn't see his eyes. You knew it was him though by his regularity and his walk. Always 9.30 on weekdays and 11.30 at the weekend. Always the same steady pace and long-legged stride.

He gave them packs of bread and cheese, delivered in small brown paper carriers and padded out with old newspapers. The people living under the railway bridges would use the paper to keep them warm at night.

"You know it's an offence to wear a hoody like that, don't you, on the streets of Citiville," said the police officer.

Our hooded friend pointed to the people under the bridge. "This is the real offence," he said. "Against humanity. Think on it now." His voice was as sweet as honey.

Bookaholic 3

25 October 2016

I just do not want this book, he thought. Why are you trying to sell it to me? Best-selling author. What does that even mean? Who says so?

He used to love Twitter for the power of the retweet. It often went past the six handshakes. Now, though, it just seemed to be book promotion after book promotion.

"That's what you get for following so many other writers," said his wife. "How do you choose your books anyway?" She laughed. "Not that you need to. What was it? 257 on your Kindle. Fifty in hard copy in the bedroom. You're getting on a bit. Will you even have time to read them all?"

Yes. She was right. Wait a minute though. This actually looked good. Despite the dull cover.

He clicked through to Amazon and then pressed the one-click button.

Wedding Flowers

26 October 2016

Two dozen very pink roses, tied together with a white satin bow, left on the step.

"Just from some well-wisher," said her chief bridesmaid. "They'll look perfect with your dress."

So they would. So much nicer than the almost failed sweet peas her brother had offered. This wedding was on a budget.

"You look fab, sis," he said as he got ready to walk her down the aisle.

Her hear leapt as they moved towards the groom and his best man who were staring wide-eyed at her. Members of the congregation turned and smiled.

This was her day.

Suddenly she felt dizzy. Pain shot up her arms and into her chest. As she fell to the floor she saw her former lover leaving the church with a smirk on his face.

It must be the roses, was her final thought.

Politics

27 October 2016

He said she covered up her husband's mistakes by telling the other women to keep Mum. She said he was a bigot and a bully. He brought a new meaning to a word often associated with card games. She isn't robust enough, he said.

Then the wife of the outgoing one stepped in and said: "This isn't just politics. This is a special situation. We mustn't let this happen."

Many people are puzzled as to how he's got this far.

"The press is against me," he said. "They're colouring me purple."

"Please watch your step." Another big guy accuses the outgoing one of a cover-up. There are accusations of papers not being available. "Please watch your step."

"There's not a lot of choice," some say. "They're both a bit dodgy."

Politics eh? Who wants to play that game? Not me!

Definition of a Writer

28 October 2016

"Right, let's go round, and everybody can introduce themselves. I'll start. I'm Gary and I'm your creative writing teacher for this term. I am a published writer. There are a few postcards about my books out here at the front of the class." His bottom was perched on the edge of the desk.

"I'm Debbie," I said. "I'm an aspiring writer."

Gary jumped up from his perch.

"No, no, no. You're either a writer or you're not. If you write, you're a writer."

He looked at the rest of the class. "How many of you write?"

Hands crept up.

Gary nodded. "Daily, weekly, monthly. Two minutes a day, ten hours a week. It doesn't matter what."

More hands crept up and soon everyone was waving confidently.

He looked at me and nodded.

"I am Debbie and I'm a writer," I said.

Activist

30 October 2016

"We've got to get this film out there. It's the most important one every made."

"Why?"

"There is debilitating bureaucracy. When people are thrown out of their homes there are knock-on effects. There aren't enough houses. Families have to keep moving. It affects the kids' education. Too many people are depending on food banks. Too many people have to go on the game."

"But what can I do?"

"Watch the film. Get your mates to watch it. Sign the petition. Get your mates to sign it."

"Is it really that bad?"

"Yes. There are 3,500 people sleeping rough, over 73,000 homeless households living in temporary accommodation. More than 1.1 million three-day food supplies given out last year by Trussell Trust food banks.

"Our country is truly in crisis."

"Oh."

He filled in the form and shared it all on Facebook.

Camp

31 October 2016

It was bewildering. There was so much to do. There was sand for building castles. Some were dabbing wet colours onto white paper and making pictures of animals and flowers. Others were making towers from bricks and knocking them down again.

It was the mud she liked the look of. She wanted to plunge her hands into its coldness.

"Anything you like, Kormi," said the lady. "You choose."

She ran over to the tray and started pulling at the creamy dough.

Quickly and deftly she made the figures. Her mama and her papa. Her three brothers and her two sisters. She lined up the figures and then smiled up at the lady.

The lady ruffled her hair and kissed her head.

If only she could breathe the life back into them. But they weren't coming back. This was home now.

Veteran

1 November 2016

She pinned the red poppy on to the lapel of his jacket, next to his pin. Under his jacket, pinned across his chest, was a band of medals.

She dusted down his jacket and stroked his beard. "So smart. They've trimmed it nicely."

He pulled on his beret. Yes it would do. The parade was going to start at 2.00. He was determined to walk.

"We'll set off in about five minutes," she said. "We want to get a good parking spot."

He nodded. The blue badge ones would fill up really quickly. He knew that as he walked he would feel again every pain he'd had before, even though the leg was no longer there.

"You're sure you're oaky with this?" her eyes were full of concern.

"Of course. Let's go." He wasn't okay, though, and never would be.

The Modern Worker

22 February 2016

The black Americano served in an elegant grey mug was good. However, the women still wore jackets stuffed with shoulder pads. Were they trying to be men? But they also still had their high heels and immaculate make-up.

It's all a mask, he thought. *A pretence.*

The other male in the room wore a suit and tie. Greg hadn't owned a suit now for five years. Clients only ever saw his head and shoulders when they met in video conferences.

The other three sat at the table. Greg perched on the side and smiled benignly at his colleagues. They included him in the conversation, welcomed his ideas, in fact.

Well it was fun but he wouldn't want that too often anymore. Social media worked better He preferred Facebook and Twitter over rent-an-office any day. He got more done at home.

The New Machine

4 November 2016

It had taken Brother Joseph just over twenty years to hone his skills to this level.

What was not to like? The man he had painted looked a bit like the Abbot anyway, only his hair was not yet grey. So the Abbot when he was younger, when he was still a scribe himself. Hopefully he would like the inclusion of the winged creature who was watching him. Perhaps he would notice that the letters in the text in the picture were as neat as the ones in the manuscript itself. People just didn't realise how difficult it was to get that shade of blue right.

The door to the studio opened.

"Brother Joseph, come quickly. It's here."

He had to obey.

The Abbot caressed the new printing machine. "Just think, every family will now be able to enjoy books."

Trick or Treat

6 November 2016

Everybody seemed to believe in her now. The children had their few hours of glory. They'd dressed as one of her kind or as vampires, zombies and archenemies of the super heroes. They'd gone from door to door. "Trick or treat," they'd called cheerfully when the doors had opened. Did anyone ever go for a "trick", she'd wondered. Ah. Perhaps she should show them soon. They'd all gone home again shortly afterwards, bags and hats full of sweet treats.

It was good to be able to go about in her proper dress.

Monday this time, with All Souls day on Tuesday. Four days, then. It was also oaky to get it out again the next weekend when they'd burn Guy Fawkes and Donald Trump. I wonder what havoc I can cause there, she thought. She stroked her wand and smiled.

Get Rich Quick

8 November 2016

Charlie clicked on the download button. Here it was: This new kit that was going to make him independent for ever.

"Cut the crap," the blurb said. "Forget all of the other hypes. My programme is the one that will make you rich."

The download took just thirty seconds.

"What are you doing?" his wife shouted up the stairs. "Shouldn't you be looking for a job?"

"I'm working."

Footsteps came up the stairs. The door opened and there stood the banshee, hand on hip.

"Another scam?"

"No, I don't think so."

She moved over and stood so that she could look at the computer screen across his shoulder.

"It's the same as all others. A waste of time and money. Do something useful."

He sighed and switched off the computer. One day he would follow through and show her.

Clouds

8 November 2016

The kids had written that they liked ice-cream, chocolate and… clouds? What did they mean? Did they mean the fluffy things in the sky? Had they actually said clowns and the lady at the Ministry of Stories had misheard? Or did they mean that record of what was on your computer?

"Do you like clouds?" she asked the boy. His tongue was poking out as he concentrated on forming his letters.

He shook his head. "If it dies on your computer it dies in the cloud as well."

There you had it. This kid couldn't write but he knew about computers.

"What about you?" she said to the little girls on the same table.

"I like it when the cows puff out clouds on the cold mornings."

Both sorts then. Except she wondered where you might find cows in Hoxton.

Witchcraft

9 November 2016

There she was, back in her normal clothes; blue jeans, Norwegian knitted jumper and soft anorak. Her blond hair belied her real supernatural state. There was maybe something about the eyebrows... thick and a little demonic. No worries. The sleek blond hair countered that.

She was sitting on a log when he found her.

"Are you all right?" he asked. "We've been searching all night."

She nodded. "Stupid of me, really. I lost my way in the fog. I did manage to shelter there, though." She pointed to the half-derelict shack behind her.

"Looks like something out of Hansel and Gretel. I hope the wicked witch didn't get you."

I am the wicked witch, she thought. The meeting with the coven the night before had been spectacular. They'd succeeded too. The misogynist had all the power now. She smiled sweetly.

@ Poppies

11 November 2016

"I might just about consider a white one."

"Okay. I understand." The young soldier nodded. He did seem very nice. "But will you let me show you something before you decide?"

Well, she prided herself on having an open mind, didn't she?" She nodded.

He showed her into the cubicle and handed her the goggles. "It might feel funny at first."

She was in a mud-bathed field. There were woods close by. She could hear battle noise and curiously behind that birdsong. Despite the birds she felt the horror of it. The pictures were so vivid she felt the coldness. She could feel their fear.

"They did it for us. Wouldn't you protect your children?" His smile was irresistible.

She was a mum. Of course she would. She placed a £2.00 coin in the slot and took a red poppy.

Bombs

14 November 2016

"It still makes me feel sick when I think about it."

"Yeah, I'm still a bit nervous when I go into town. Always looking round. Could that chap over there have a bomb under his jacket? Or that one? What does think he's doing?"

"Like Birmingham in the 1970s. Nearly always a diversion here, a road block there."

"Yep. You get used to it. But when something actually goes off…"

"In Birmingham even that little bomb, days before the pub-bombings, made the floor shake in our bathroom."

"Amazing about the post box."

"Strong things, post boxes."

"They moved it and then moved it back after they'd finished rebuilding."

"Did they deliver all of the letters?"

"Not the one to my Jack, thank God."

"Why do you say that?"

"Because I was breaking up with him. He never got it."

"Cool."

Story

15 November 2016

Why would I need a book about story arcs? It's simple, really, isn't it? You just have a beginning, a middle and an end. A romantic one, for instance:

Beginning: Boy gets girl

Middle: Boy loses girl.

End: Boy gets girl back again.

What if he gets what he wants but not what he needs, though? He wants the girl but he really needs to increase his self-esteem. This one might not be good for him. That might means getting another one who understands him better. Hmm.

Gotta have a car chase. He chases after her – on his motor bike, a horse, on foot – oh I know, he's a hippy and has a VW camper van. He'd be better off with the girl in the rainbow dress only he doesn't know it yet.

Should I try a beat sheet?

A Bauble

18 November 2016

"Any ideas what you want for Christmas?" The question was routine, like everything else, totally predictable.

"What about booking a cruise?" It was something Allan had wanted to do for some time.

Mark frowned. "Can we afford it? Can you get the time off?" He reached for the remote, flicked through a few channels and settled for a wildlife film.

Allan couldn't watch. It was making him feel horny. That cupboard under the stairs needed tidying. He may as well make a start now.

There was a lot of junk there. He made three piles. Stuff to bin, stuff for the charity shop and stuff to keep. Then he found last year's winking Christmas bauble.

"Hey, time to make some magic happen," he called to Mark.

Mark laughed at the bauble. "You know what. A cruise isn't a bad idea."

Marketing Plan

20 November 2016

It was very tempting indeed. What was there to lose anyway? The company offered a money back guarantee. Would this solve his marketing problems?

The prices were reasonable. It would take him at least three hours to do the work they charged $49 for. They had more contacts as well. They could make more impact, surely? Could he afford $49 at the moment, though?

He made his way through the Frequently Asked Questions. Yes other people worried about the same things that bothered him. The answers all seemed reasonable.

They suggested three Facebook groups. He studied the details. Yes, they looked doable.

Would he remember to follow the routines, though? Along with everything else in his wonderful free-lance life?

It was no good. It was all too much. He closed the link and returned to worrying about his poor sales.

World Book Day

21 November 2016

"It will be chaos."

"The mums will get competitive."

"They won't be able to work properly dressed up like that."

"We'll have to find costumes as well. As if we haven't got enough to do."

They were hard work, the four Marys. They were as old as their names. They resented her being so young. But none of them had applied for the post of headteacher.

She took a deep breath. "The board of governors have approved and the literacy advisor thinks it's a good idea. We're all dressing up as characters from favourite books for Book Week Scotland. We can review it afterwards."

The following Monday the school was populated by Alices, witches, fairies and Potter boys."

"It is a bit of lark," said one of the Marys. All four of them had dressed as their namesakes from *Bunty*.

Accounting

7 December 2016

Her hair was immaculate, straight and sleek, bobbling with suggested health. It hadn't been cheap. They expected that at the agency, though. They'd made it very clear: "No small town also-rans. Only a top city salon."

"We have to do it, Mum," she'd said. "Look at it as investment."

"Well you'd better keep a spread sheet of all that you're costing and all that you're earning."

Her mother never gave up being an accountant.

She gazed again at her reflection. She couldn't help grinning. That was the other thing: the amount they'd spent on getting her teeth white and straight. Her make-up too was perfect. This was definitely the look.

"Can I see the report?" she asked.

"No, sweetheart. It's brutal."

"What do you mean?"

The receptionist sighed. "Basically, you're too stereotyped. You look too much like Miss Cover Girl."

Phone Call

8 December 2016

You should always stand up to make important phone calls – even if you stayed in your pyjamas until noon and the people couldn't see you anyway.

Better go all of the way with this one. She washed her hair, putting it through a blond rinse. She tongued it then and created soft bouncy curls. She put on some false lashes and a pale blue eye shadow. She outlined her lids in a soft brown. Nothing but bright red would do for her lips.

It had to be the pink telephone in the sitting room. She dialled the number and held her breath as she waited for him to pick up.

She didn't wait for him to speak. "It's over Ray. It's a step too far this time. You're out by five today or I'll instruct my lawyers." She'd done it.

Silly Jumper Day

23 December 2016

It still didn't feel much like Christmas. Today's work was still on the floor. Galley proofs from ten days ago were yet to be checked. She needed to send out ten review copies. She mustn't forget the rejections. Still it was at least likely that the recipients wouldn't get them until early next year.

She'd dared to wear her red jumper with the big Christmas pudding on it today, though. As yet no one had made any negative remarks.

Roddy, the office joker, grinned at her. "Is that water in your glass?" he asked.

She sighed. "Too right."

"You sure about that? Try it."

She took a sip. It tasted of cherries and almonds and alcohol.

"You like?"

She nodded. He snapped with his phone. "Say cheese. Merry Christmas, Cindy."

Suddenly it was beginning to feel a lot like Christmas.

Tap-dancing

29 December 2016

That's not their feet making that noise, she thought as she watched the clip of the actress who had died a few days after her daughter. "Anyway, these old Hollywood films were just an excuse for a lot of singing and dancing." Tap-dancing in particular, she thought. She remembered the floor of the cottage that they'd stayed in over Christmas. That would be good for tap-dancing, she thought.

She watched the clip twice. It's so bad it's good, she thought. She admired their energy. She wondered why the men had to cover their legs but it was okay for the girl to show hers blatantly.

It was a good story, though.

She resisted watching it one more time and wondered how long it would be before they showed *Star Wars* and *Singing in the Rain*.

"Bring it on," she whispered.

Time Slip

30 December 2016

It had been heady, close and clammy and now a sudden cold front arrived. The sky blackened and a wind sprung up. Within seconds the sea seemed to boil and the waves grew to over ten feet.

"How can that be?" said Jed.

"I've never seen anything like it," said Arthur.

"Global warming," muttered Carmen.

A black tornado skimmed across the water and turned into a water spout.

Then just as soon as it had all started it stopped and there was calm once more. An eerie silence followed. Jed pointed.

"This isn't where we were," said Arthur.

Facing them was a strange vessel steered by an old man in long robes.

"It must be some sort of time-slip," whispered Carmen. She looked directly at the old man. "Which year is it?"

"The year of our Lord 200," he replied.

Initiation

7 January 2017

She had the costume. The blue silk strappy dress and matching cloak set off her sleek long blond hair. Her eyes sparkled with excitement. She had carefully pencilled her eyebrows, and lined and coloured her lids. Her lips were outlined in black and coloured purple. Yes, she was a demon all right. Would she pass the initiation test? And get through the fifteen stages?

The Dragon Master smiled. "Very fetching, my dear. Now show me your act."

She turned towards him and pouted. She jangled her hands and was relieved to feel the rush of warmth as the fire spread from her elbows, down through her arms and out through her fingers until the jumping flames lit up the dark.

"Splendid, splendid," whispered the Dragon Master, his voice hoarse with excitement. Fire was coming out on his breath. Result indeed!

We Have Lift-Off

8 January 2016

The beast was ready. Her sleek orange and white body glistened in the sunlight. Such clean colours suited her.

"This is it then," said Arnold.

Jeff nodded.

Both men put on their safety helmets. The material of the special space suits crackled as they walked nervously up the steps leading to the cockpit.

The two men took their seats and started the initial checks.

"All clear," said Arnold at last.

"Second that," said Jeff.

The engines gained power. She lifted gently and swung out of the hangar. Soon they were above the clouds and then out of Earth's atmosphere.

They gazed out of the window at the blue planet.

"Worth all those years of crowd-funding and technical hitches."

"Oh yes." Jeff pulled out the throttle and they hurtled towards Mars. It would be years before they got back home.

A Third Way

5 January 2017

The Little People on Great Union Island were arguing.

"I want to live on Great Union, not Little Albinium," said one.

"Great Union will be great if we cut our ties with Contentia."

"You want to go back to all those squabbles between the groups on Contentia? After all those years of peace?"

"What about the wishes of the Northern Lands, and the Northern Island?"

"Or even Womensville, Kidneylake, Hairtuft and Gainwich? Not to mention Westchurch?"

"We'd be free to trade with the whole world."

"If they'll have us."

"Stop," shouted Buddy. "There's a third way. Let's put our energies into creating One World."

They all stopped talking and stared.

"It would never work," mumbled one or two.

Buddy stood up. "Compromise means no one wins. Win, win, win is possible."

Twenty years later our One World came into existence.

NHS

16 January 2017

Elsie fell, catching her knee on the cobbled path. She heard something crack.

"Are you all right?" a young woman asked.

"I think I've done something to my knee," said Elsie.

"Oh, we'd better get you along to A & E."

"But the doctors' surgery is just there."

The young woman shook her head. "It'll need an X-Ray and they don't have machine at the Health Centre."

"You're going all the way into town? Wouldn't the Cottage Hospital do."

The other woman shook her head. "Closed for small injuries the other week."

Six hours later Elsie was moved to a bed on a ward. That was after two hours waiting for triage and the other four lying on a trolley in a corridor. At least they'd given her some pain-killers. The young woman had long since gone home.

Reluctant Mistress

25 January 2017

The sun was going down, bathing the shore opposite in pink light. You could convince yourself it was the sea. Waves danced on the surface of the water and the shore was just about sandy.

Where had all those years gone? It seemed like just a couple.

She turned to look at him. He was still recognisable. It had taken just second to see beyond the grey hair and the crinkles.

"You haven't change a bit," he'd said when they'd met. They'd kissed.

Well she knew she looked young for her age and she also knew that is exactly the sort of thing he would say.

This ought to be romantic. The place was well-kept and the nearby restaurant, once a student dive, had now gone upmarket.

All she wanted to do, though, was get away as quickly as possible.

Prepared

27 January 2017

The first hurdle of course was always getting up in the morning. It was such a bore. She wished she had magical powers and could just click her fingers to produce herself, showered, perfumed and dressed with hair styled and make-up on.

No matter, she had to go through the routine and Classic FM helped.

Here she was. The moment of truth. She looked in the mirror.

Yes, that would do nicely. Blond curls framed her round face. You couldn't see the makeup but you could see its effect. She raised an eyebrow and smiled to herself. There was a lot to do today.

She would be hiding in the sewer outlet as the convey rode past. The gun was safely stowed in her handbag. It would be a messy job. Important to look her best, though. Bring it on.

Green

19 February 2017

She couldn't remember the dream, not quite. Except that it did prove that she dreamed in colour. The dream had been green. Pale green. She closed her eyelids again. No it wasn't just the colour that she saw then. That was a mixture of purple and orange. Was green the complement?

The shape was interesting too. It was a little like spiders' webs. Or were they strings of snot? Wait. Hadn't there been something right in the middle? An egg, or something? Or maybe the spider's prey?

She must hurry. Time was short. Anti-bullying day at college today. The neuroscientist would tell them what happened in the brains of the bully and of the victim. She was to talk of how the synapses worked, of how the bully preyed upon its victim and of how he was green with envy.

Blue

10 March 2017

He'd been in the force over ten years and it still shocked him. Every time he had to be careful not to vomit. That wouldn't do: not in front of the younger chaps and the women. Not to mention the general public.

The familiar blue line: Police Line Do Not Cross. Blue because the police were blue. The boys in blue, didn't they say?

What was it then? One murder and one attempted murder? Maybe one suicide?

At least the child was unharmed.

He hoped it had been an intruder. Sad, yes, the father – he supposed the man was the child's father – was dead and maybe the mother was injured because she'd fought the intruder bravely.

The WPC was taking the child way now. A crowd had gathered.

"Please move on, ladies and gents," he said. "Nothing to see here."

Skulls

11 March 2017

The skull had remains of blood seeming to drip from the eye sockets and was painted white at the bottom. Was it what she thought it was? She snapped off the light. Yes, where the white paint had been now glowed a sort of yellowy green. The teeth were remarkably well preserved but not quite straight.

Her assistant came and tapped her on the shoulder. "Ma'am, there's a report of another case. Twenty miles away at Little Hatton. Seems the victim may have died about ten hours after this chap. He also left a skull behind."

"Making assumptions, aren't we, Jones?"

"Sorry, Ma'am, but normally…."

She looked over her spectacles at him. He nodded and scurried away.

The real pain was that some had stolen her idea. Was somebody on to her? She would just have to be more careful.

Also By Chapeltown Books

January Stones
by Gill James

These stories were written one a day throughout January 2013. They were originally published on a blog called Gill's January Stones. Sometimes the stories would come right at the beginning of the day. Sometimes they would take a while longer.

Do they have a theme? Not really, though the idea of 'stones' is one of turning them over slowly on the beach until we find the right one.

There was no strict word count. Each story is as long as it needs to be. It had to be finished, though, by midnight of that day.

Order from Amazon:

ISBN: 978-1-910542-10-1 (paperback)
978-1-910542-11-8 (ebook)

Chapeltown Books

Paisley Shirt
by Gail Aldwin

Paisley Shirt is a fascinating collection of 27 stories that reveal the extraordinary nature of people and places. Through a variety of characters and voices, these stories lay bare the human experience and what it is like to live in our world.

"I really enjoyed every one of Gail Aldwin's perfectly-formed little stories, and was hooked from the very first one." (*Amazon*)

Order from Amazon:
ISBN: 978-1-910542-29-3 (paperback)
978-1-910542-30-9 (ebook)

Chapeltown Books

Brightly Coloured Horses
by Mandy Huggins

Twenty-seven tales of betrayal and loss, of dreams and hopes, of lovers, liars and cheats. Stories with a strong sense of place, transporting us from the seashore to the city, from India's monsoon to the heat of Cuba, and from the supermarket aisle to a Catalonian fiesta. We meet a baby that never existed, a car called Marilyn, a one-eyed cat, and a boy whose kisses taste of dunked biscuits.

"A masterclass in flash fiction" (*Amazon*)

Order from Amazon:
ISBN: 978-1-910542-19-4 (paperback)
978-1-910542-20-0 (ebook)

Chapeltown Books

Clara's Story: a Holocaust Biography
by Gill James

Clara will not be daunted. Her life will not end when her beloved husband dies too young. She will become a second mother to the young children who live away from home at a rather special school – a particular class of disabled children growing up in Nazi Germany.

Clara's Story: a Holocaust Biography is the second story in the Schellberg Cycle. It might be described as a tragedy or it might be described as a story of survival. In the end it is up to the reader or even Clara herself to decide.

Order from Amazon:
ISBN: 978-1-910542-33-0 (paperback)
978-1-910542-34-7 (ebook)

Chapeltown Books